W9-BRP-136

For Claire and Jack,
they could have written this book themselves,
but they were too busy playing —L. U.

For the unmovable A. J. H. —H. H.

Text copyright © 2018 by Linda Urban.
Illustrations copyright © 2018 by Hadley Hooper.
All rights reserved.
No part of this book may be reproduced in any form
without written permission from the publisher.

Library of Congress Cataloging-in-Publication Data:

Names: Urban, Linda, author. | Hooper, Hadley, illustrator.
Title: Mabel and Sam at home / by Linda Urban ; illustrated by Hadley Hooper.
Description: San Francisco : Chronicle Books, [2018] | Summary: Mabel and her
younger brother Sam approach their new home and the trauma of moving by
turning it into an adventure, imagining they are sailors approaching a new
land, tour guides exploring a museum, and finally astronauts in space.
Identifiers: LCCN 2017006125| ISBN 9781452139968 (alk. paper) |
ISBN 1452139962 (alk. paper)
Subjects: LCSH: Moving, Household—Juvenile fiction. | Brothers and
sisters—Juvenile fiction. | Imagination—Juvenile fiction. |
Dwellings—Juvenile fiction. | CYAC: Moving, Household--Fiction. |
Brothers and sisters—Fiction. | Imagination—Fiction. |
Dwellings—Fiction. | LCGFT: Picture books.
Classification: LCC PZ7.U637 Mab 2018 | DDC [E]--dc23
LC record available at https://lccn.loc.gov/2017006125

Manufactured in China.

Design by Kristine Brogno.
Typeset in Ernestine Pro.
The illustrations in this book were created
by using tradition printmaking techniques
and finished in Photoshop.

10 9 8 7 6 5 4 3 2

Chronicle Books LLC
680 Second Street
San Francisco, California 94107

Chronicle Books—we see things differently.
Become part of our community at www.chroniclekids.com.

Mabel and Sam at Home

By LINDA URBAN   Illustrated by HADLEY HOOPER

chronicle books · san francisco

ON THE HIGH SEAS

At the new house, there were movers and shouting
and boxes and blankets.

FRAGILE

There were chairs where chairs did not go
and sofas where sofas could not stay.

HANDLE
WITH CARE

There were many places a girl like Mabel and a boy like Sam could be tripped over or smooshed or trod upon. There was one safe place where they would not be.

And that is how Mabel became a Sea Captain.

HANDLE
WITH CARE

"Ahoy!" said Captain Mabel. "Welcome aboard the Handle with Care. I am the captain."

"And I am Ahoy," said Ahoy.

"You're not Ahoy. Ahoy means hello. You are First Mate Sam."

"What does First Mate mean?" asked First Mate Sam.

"It means you get to follow orders,"
said Captain Mabel. "Swab the deck!"

First Mate Sam swabbed.

"Hoist the sail on the mizzen mast,"
said Captain Mabel.

First Mate Sam hoisted.

"Go left," Captain Mabel commanded.

HANDLE
WITH CARE

HANDLE WITH CARE

And they were off, sailing left on the high seas.

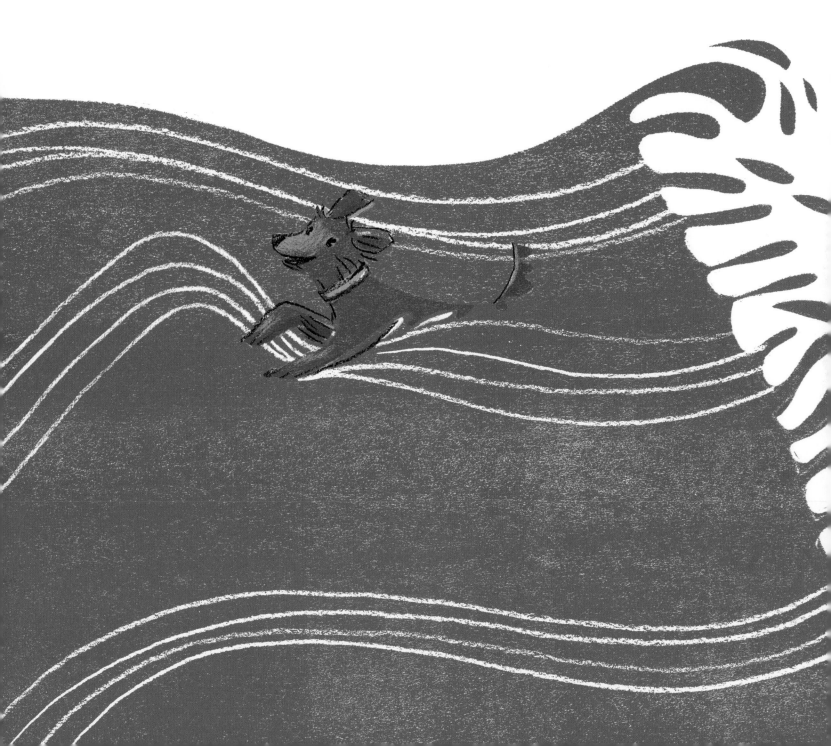

The seas were rough and full of danger.

Captain Mabel saw pirates

and whales

and sea serpents.

"As long as we stay on board, I am in command and we are safe," said Captain Mabel. "Don't worry."

"I'm not worried," said First Mate Sam.

"You are," said Captain Mabel. "You are just too scared to know it."

"Are you worried?" asked First Mate Sam.

"Of course not," said Captain Mabel. "I am the captain."

"Maybe you are too scared to know it, too."

"The Captain knows everything," said Captain Mabel. "I know I am not worried."

"What else do you know?" asked First Mate Sam.

"I know that when you are worried it is best to keep busy."

Captain Mabel kept First Mate Sam busy.

She ordered him to swab more things.

She ordered him to fish for halibut.

She ordered him to keep lookout.

That is when First Mate Sam spotted an island.

"Land ho!" he called. He lowered anchor. "Let's go!" he said.

"You don't say 'let's go,' you say 'all ashore,'" said Captain Mabel. "And you don't say it at all. I do. I'm the captain."

First Mate Sam waited for Captain Mabel to say "all ashore," but she did not.

HANDLE WITH CARE

"Land is full of unknown dangers,"
said Captain Mabel.

"Weren't we on land before?"
asked First Mate Sam.

"It was different land," said Captain Mabel.
"Don't worry. We are safe on board."

They stayed on board and they stayed on board and they did not leave the ship.

The seas calmed. The pirates vanished.

HANDLE WITH CARE

There was nothing to see in the sea.

There was nothing new to swab or hoist.

The fishing was poor.

But Captain Mabel did not budge.

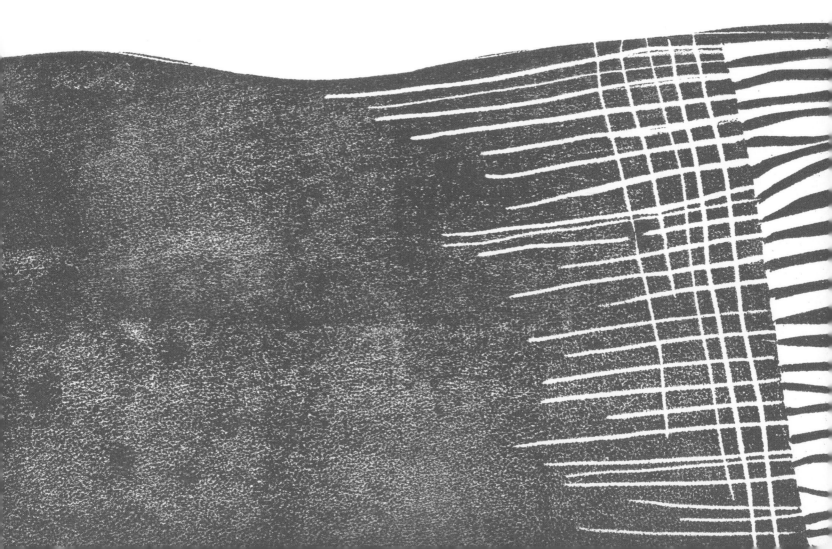

Then First Mate Sam heard a sound. A rumbling sound.

"What was that?" asked First Mate Sam.

"Nothing," said Captain Mabel.

"Something," said First Mate Sam.

"It was a sea serpent," said Captain Mabel.

"I'm hungry," said First Mate Sam.

"Look," said First Mate Sam. "People!"

"Those are inhabitants," said Captain Mabel.

"What are inhabitants?"

"People. People who live someplace."

"The inhabitants have pizza," said First Mate Sam.

"They might be dangerous," said Captain Mabel.

"Starving might be dangerous, too," said First Mate Sam.

Captain Mabel looked at the inhabitants bearing pizza. They did not seem as dangerous as sea serpents.

HANDLE WITH CARE

"Okay," she said. "All ashore."

First Mate Sam did not hear.

He was already heading for land,
"ahoying" at the inhabitants.

AT THE MUSEUM

"Is that a new chair?" asked Sam.

"No," said Mabel. "That is the lullaby chair."

"It looks different,"
said Sam.

It did look different.

At the before house, the lullaby chair always stood in front of the yellow wall and rocked on the mossy green rug. Now the lullaby chair looked like a stranger.

But it wasn't.

Sam just needed reminding.

And that is how Mabel became a Tour Guide.

"Welcome to the New House Museum, ladies and gentlemen," said Tour Guide Mabel.

"No ladies," said Sam. "Just me, the gentleman."

"Shhhhhh," said Mabel. "You have to whisper inside the museum. Out of respect for the other visitors." Mabel pointed her umbrella at Mr. Woofie.

"Oh," whispered Sam.

Sam followed Tour Guide Mabel into the living room.

"Behold!" she said.

"Be what?" asked Sam.

"Behold!" said Mabel. "That means 'look at this!'"

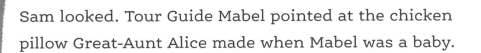

Sam looked. Tour Guide Mabel pointed at the chicken pillow Great-Aunt Alice made when Mabel was a baby.

"This is the Ancient Chicken of Cleveland. It is an important artifact," said Mabel.

"What's an artifact?" asked Sam.

"A thing. It is an important thing."

Sam nodded. "Why is it important?"

"Because it is old," said Mabel. "The older you are, the more important you are."

"Oh," said Sam.

Sam followed Tour Guide Mabel to the kitchen.

"Behold!" she said, pointing to the table.

"I'm beholding. That's Grandma's old table," said Sam. "Nice artifact."

"This is the famous table where the Peanut Butter and Chocolate Chip Sandwich was invented," said Mabel.

"I eat those," said Sam.

"Yes," said Mabel. "But you ate them second. Museums are about people who do things first."

"You ate them first," said Sam.

"Why, yes. Yes, I did," said Mabel.

Famous Sandwich do not Touch!

Pea
Butt

Tour Guide Mabel led Sam to the next exhibit.

"Do you know what this is?" asked Mabel.

"My Bunny Wubby," said Sam.

"It is a Mississippi Wishing Rabbit. They are very rare."

"Oh," said Sam.

"Petting its ears brings seven years' good luck," said Mabel.

"Really?" asked Sam.

"No touching," said Mabel.

"You're touching," said Sam.

"I am the tour guide. I am not touching. I am demonstrating."

"Oh," said Sam.

"Let's move on," said Tour Guide Mabel.

"Wait," said Sam. "What about this artifact here?"

"That is not an artifact," said Mabel.
"That is a frosted pitty-pat."

"It is the Ancient Frosted Pitty-Pat of Calimari,"
said Sam. "The last one of its kind."

"Oh," said Mabel.

"And I am the first to discover it," said Sam.

"I see," said Mabel.

"Do you?" asked Sam. "Not everyone can see its pitty-pat goodness."

"I do see it," said Mabel.

"No touching," said Sam. He licked his fingers. "I am demonstrating the goodness."

IN SPACE

After supper, Mabel and Sam were astronauts.

"Blast off!" said Astronaut Sam.

"We blasted off a long time ago," said Astronaut Mabel.

"We are already in space and I am already driving."

"Oh," said Astronaut Sam. "Blast on then."

Astronaut Mabel blasted on.

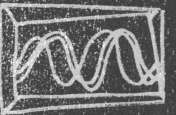

Astronaut Mabel sent Astronaut Sam on a space walk.

"Whoa!" said Astronaut Sam. "Meteors!"

"I've got you covered," said Astronaut Mabel.

"I've got me covered, too," said Astronaut Sam.

They were Mabel's covers and they were red. Sam's covers were blue. At the before house, they were each on a different bed in the same room. Now, Sam's covers were on a different bed in a different room way, way down the hall.

Astronaut Mabel pulled Astronaut Sam back inside the ship.
"Did you see anything out there?" she asked.

"I saw lots of things out there," said Astronaut Sam.
"Out there is where everything is."

"Where are we going now?" asked Astronaut Sam.

"We are going to the Planet Perfecto," said Astronaut Mabel.

"Why?" asked Astronaut Sam.

"Because we are bold," said Astronaut Mabel.

"That is true," said Astronaut Sam.
"But weren't we bold before?"

"We were bold, but not Space Bold.
Space Bold is bigger, because space is bigger."

"Oh," said Astronaut Sam.

"Also, our old planet was getting crowded,"
said Astronaut Mabel. "We needed space to explore.
We needed space to think."

Astronaut Sam did not know you needed space to think.
"I think in my head," he said. "There is plenty of space in there."

Astronaut Mabel and Astronaut Sam zipped through space.

They dodged asteroids and chased comets.

For a while, their rocket made a zooming sound as they drove, and then, eventually, it didn't.

Night snuck up on space.

It got darker and darker.

Space got bigger.

"Maybe there is too much space in space,"
said Astronaut Sam.

Finally, Mom plugged in the moon.

There was just enough light to make a landing.

"Is this the Planet Perfecto?" asked Astronaut Sam.

Astronaut Mabel looked around. The new planet
was surprisingly homey. "Could be," she said.
"We'll need to do some exploring to be sure."

"Time for bed, Bold Astronauts," said Dad.

Astronaut Sam climbed out of Mabel's rocket.

He looked

      way,

         way

            down the hallway.

aarrooooo

"Did you hear that?" asked Sam.

"I think it is an alien," said Astronaut Mabel.

"I think Mr. Woofie needs to go outside," said Dad.

"Maybe Sam should stay near the rocket tonight,"
said Astronaut Mabel. "Just in case."

"Maybe all of us should stay near the rocket tonight," said Sam.

"You could sleep in the ship,"
said Astronaut Mabel.

"Just for tonight?" said the Astronaut Parents.

"Just for tonight," said Mabel and Sam.

"We will sleep under the stars," said Astronaut Sam.

Astronaut Mom let Mr. Woofie outside. And back inside.

Astronaut Dad found Sam's blue covers and tucked his space children in, snug under the stars.

The new planet was cozy and mostly quiet. Mr. Woofie paced.

"He is exploring," said Astronaut Mabel.

"He can't find his rug," said Astronaut Sam.

Astronaut Mabel whistled. "Come here, Bold Space Dog," she said.

Mr. Woofie click-clacked into base and onto Astronaut Mabel's covers.

"He can explore tomorrow," said Astronaut Sam as the bold space dog squeezed between them.

"Tomorrow," said Mabel, "we will all explore and be bold. Tomorrow we will be even bolder than we are today."

Sam said nothing. He was asleep.

And then, so was Mabel.